LITTLE JACK RABBITS' ADVENTURES

"Don't wear out my mat."

He tiptoed up behind them.

"I feel lots better now."

Giving ten carrot pennies to the monkey.

LITTLE JACK RABBIT'S
ADVENTURES

LITTLE JACK RABBIT BOOKS

(Trademark Registered)

BY

DAVID CORY

Little Jack Rabbit Hid Behind His Mother's Skirt.

Little Jack Rabbit's Adventures. *Frontispiece*—(*Page* 16)

LITTLE JACK RABBIT BOOKS
(Trademark Registered)

LITTLE JACK RABBIT'S ADVENTURES

BY

DAVID CORY

Author of
LITTLE JACK RABBIT AND DANNY FOX
LITTLE JACK RABBIT AND THE SQUIRREL BROTHERS
LITTLE JACK RABBIT AND CHIPPY CHIPMUNK
LITTLE JACK RABBIT AND THE BIG BROWN BEAR

ILLUSTRATED BY
H. S. BARBOUR

NEW YORK
GROSSET & DUNLAP
PUBLISHERS
Made in the United States of America

CONTENTS

Contents

LITTLE JACK RABBIT'S ADVENTURES

THE RAILROAD

IT was a wild story that came to the ears of Little Jack Rabbit for, as he came hopping down the Shady Forest Path, a whole troop of his playmates ran out to meet him, and one cried one thing, and one another, but the words which he heard most plainly were:

"The railroad! The railroad! Oh, have you heard?"

"Yes," answered Little Jack Rabbit, not at all excited, "I know a railroad is going to run past the Sunny Meadow."

"Oh, but that's nothing! It's going to

run right through your house!" cried Busy Beaver.

"Right through the Old Bramble Patch!" shouted Chippy Chipmunk.

"Right through your front door!" screamed Gray Squirrel.

"I don't believe that," said Little Jack Rabbit. "A railroad can't get through a door!"

"Why, of course they'll take out the door," replied Busy Beaver; "they'll pull down your whole house; they'll clear away the Old Bramble Patch; why, they may use the whole of the Sunny Meadow—every bit of it!"

By this time Little Jack Rabbit was excited. Already he saw the dear Old Bramble Patch torn out by the roots; the little house gone, and himself and all the family

forced to rove homeless through the Shady
Forest. So it was no wonder he almost forgot to stop at the postoffice on his way home.

But as he came up the Shady Forest Path
that afternoon, he saw that the dear Old
Bramble Patch was still there—that was
one comfort. No wandering about tonight,
at least.

"And there, too, was his little brother,
Bobby Tail, turning somersaults under the
Old Chestnut Tree, and Mr. and Mrs. John
Rabbit sitting quietly on the front doorstep.

So Little Jack Rabbit plucked up heart
and asked Papa Rabbit if the railroad were
going to take away the Old Bramble Patch
and their house.

"No, it isn't," replied Mr. Rabbit, "but
it's coming mighty close."

"I just knew it wasn't," said Little Jack

Rabbit with a sigh of relief. "But Busy
Beaver said it was and that I must·pack up
my clothes at once."

"Well, the line was laid out to run right
through the dear Old Bramble Patch," said
Mr. Rabbit, "but when they found it must
cross the Old Duck Pond, they turned it to
one side. So the dear Old Bramble Patch
is safe."

THE FIRST TRAIN

Look out for the Choo-choo cars!
Don't you hear the thunder jars?
First the whistle, then the bell
Clanging through the Forest Dell.

FOR weeks and weeks there was great excitement among the Little People of the Shady Forest and Sunny Meadow. From behind trees and bushes, rocks and stumps, they watched the building of the railroad.

Professor Jim Crow came to offer advice, but changed his mind. As for Little Jack Rabbit, he looked out from behind a stump and wondered.

Cousin Cotton Tail had been forced to move from the Big Brush Heap on the hill.

She and her little bunnies were now visiting in the Old Bramble Patch.

When Little Jack Rabbit was told that a railroad must be level, he thought a man would come with a big scythe and slice off the top of the hill like a loaf of bread and lay the slices in the hollows.

This wasn't so very strange, seeing that he was only a little bunny boy and, of course, didn't know anything about building railroads.

Every day the railroad came nearer being finished. The hill was dug out. As Mr. Mole remarked, "It was done almost as well as I could have done it, only, of course, I would have made a tunnel."

Then the sleepers were laid. Busy Beaver smiled as he watched the men lay the great logs on the smooth earth.

"Wouldn't they be dandy for my dam?" he remarked.

"You've got all you need," answered Little Jack Rabbit. "I'm glad they didn't break up the Old Rail Fence and make railroad ties out of it."

Finally the rails were fastened on the logs and the railroad was finished; the first train was to run through and everybody was waiting to see it.

Mr. and Mrs. John Rabbit put on their Sunday clothes and took Little Jack Rabbit and Brother Bobby Tail to the end of the Old Rail Fence.

Pretty soon a black speck appeared at the end of the long line. It grew bigger and bigger. A cloud of smoke arose and drifted over to the Shady Forest. There was a rattle and a roar and a din. Little

Jack Rabbit hid behind his mother's skirt, but the train had already passed them.

And there on the platform of the last car, stood the Farmer's Boy, holding on by the door, bowing and smiling and proud as a king.

A NARROW ESCAPE

Hear the engine whistle toot!
See the smoke and smell the soot!
Lucky that the train don't stay,
But flashes by and far away!

At first the Grown-ups in the Shady Forest and the Sunny Meadow were very sorry to have the railroad come so near, but after a while they found it didn't matter so much; for the cars passed through a "cut" so deep that the engine's smokestack hardly reached the top, and you only knew they were there by the sound.

Of course, it took Cousin Cotton Tail ever and ever so long to get used to the Old

Bramble Patch. You see, it wasn't anything like the Old Brush Heap, with its covering of trailing vines, and she was glad when she was able to go back to her old home on the other side of the Bubbling Brook.

On this side the Sunny Meadow was just the same; so was the Shady Forest, and by and by everybody almost forgot that there had been a time when there wasn't any railroad.

At the Old Barnyard, however, things were very different, for the railroad made a turn just there and came in very close to the Big Red Barn.

Cocky Doodle had all he could do to keep the Barnyard Folk out of danger. Every morning after his early cock-a-doodle-do he read them a lesson on the dangers of crossing railroad tracks.

For a while Henny Penny laid her eggs in the Henhouse. The truth was that her nest in the corner of the Old Rail Fence happened to be just at the end of the Sunny Meadow where the railroad ran through the "cut," and the noise of the cars made her nervous.

Ducky Waddles was glad that the Old Duck Pond was still safe. He had heard how it had just escaped being bridged over for the noisy cars.

Yes, everyone kept away from the railroad track except Goosey Lucy. And why Goosey Lucy liked to waddle down the steep bank and along the hard wooden logs of the roadbed no one could find out.

But one fine day Goosey Lucy got caught. Yes, sir. Before she could get off the track the train came along. It was very narrow between the two steep banks, and she couldn't fly high enough to reach the top. Cocky Doodle and Henny Penny shut their eyes. They couldn't bear to see what was going to happen.

But Goosey Lucy wasn't such a goose, after all. She sat perfectly still between the rails, and when the train had passed over her, she got up, shook the cinders off her white feathers and waddled back to the Old Barnyard!

SCHOOL

"COME, get your cap, I'm going to take you to school today!"

Little Jack Rabbit was too surprised to answer—he just opened his mouth, and the only sound his mother heard was a funny little noise like a whistle.

"Don't you hear me?" she asked, tying the strings of her Sunday bonnet under her furry chin.

"Whew!" said the little rabbit at last recovering from his surprise. "Why do you want me to go to school?"

"Because all the Shady Forest grown-ups think it's a good thing to have a school for

21

the children," and she gave her bonnet a push and pulled on her black silk mitts.

"Get your cap. Every mother will be there for the opening day, and we mustn't be late."

The little rabbit hopped silently along by his mother's side, wondering how it had all happened so suddenly. He hadn't heard a word about a school, nor had any of his playmates.

"Why didn't you tell me sooner?" he asked at last.

"Because we didn't want Grandmother Magpie to know anything until the matter was settled," answered Mrs. Rabbit in a low voice. "She is such a busy-body."

Goodness me! Mrs. Rabbit had hardly finished speaking when up flew the very

person she had been talking about. Yes,
there she stood, right on the Shady Forest
Path a few feet in front of them.

"Good morning," said Grandmother
Magpie.

Mrs. Jack Rabbit gave her bonnet strings
a jerk. She always did this when she was
angry, and the sight of that disagreeable
bird reminded her of the time she had told
tales on Little Jack Rabbit.

"Good morning," answered the little rabbit's mother stiffly. She didn't really want
to say good morning, but she had to be
polite.

"Where are you going?" asked Grandmother Magpie, hopping along by Mrs.
Rabbit's side. Mrs. Rabbit said nothing,
only hopped along faster, but she couldn't

get rid of that mischievous old bird. Oh,
my, no. She stuck around like a chestnut
burr.

"Grandmother Magpie," said Mrs. Rabbit at last, "I have some important business
to attend to this morning, so I will say
goodby." And she gave Grandmother Mischief, as she was often called, such a stiff
bow that the old lady magpie stopped short
and let them go on without her.

A MISTAKE IN SPELLING

THE Shady Forest School had once been a pigeon house, but when the farm was sold and the old buildings torn down, it had been left to shelter Mr. and Mrs. Pigeon, who wouldn't move away.

One night during a great storm it had toppled off the post on which it stood, and rolled down the hillside, helped along by Billy Breeze, until it had landed on the edge of the Shady Forest.

Here it had been discovered by the Little Forest Folk, and at Parson Owl's suggestion, had been pushed and shoved in and out among the trees until it stood right-side up in a sunlit clearing.

25

Then Parson Owl had called together all
the Grown-ups and persuaded them to
make it into a schoolhouse.

And, well, here we are with Mrs. Rabbit
and her little bunny on their way to the
opening exercises, so there is no need of
saying anything more about it, except that
it had a nice door in front and a dozen
round holes, under which were fastened
little pieces of board for wide windowsills,
on which the pigeons used to stand and
preen their feathers.

As Little Jack Rabbit and his mother
drew near they saw Chippy Chipmunk's
face at one of the little round windows.
Then Busy Beaver looked out of another,
and pretty soon every little round window
had a head peeping through, while in the

doorway stood Professor Jim Crow in his black swallowtail coat.

"Good morning, Mrs. Rabbit," he said, looking over his spectacles. "You have brought another scholar, I see."

When they were seated in the schoolroom, he walked over to the big blackboard.

"John," he said, turning to the little rabbit, "tell me how to spell your name."

Goodness gracious me! Would you believe it, the little rabbit answered "J-A-C-K!" You see, he was so used to being called just "Jack" that he spelt "John" the same way.

Then Professor Jim Crow asked who was the first President, but he didn't enquire who was going to be the next, for I guess

he thought the little rabbit hadn't studied
Politics enough.　After that he told Mrs.
Rabbit that she had a very bright little
bunny boy even if he didn't know how to
spell his right name.

DISOBEDIENT JIMMY CROW

PROFESSOR JIM CROW and his family lived in the Tall Pine Tree.

"Now, Mrs. Crow," he said to his wife one morning, "as I shall be away almost all day teaching the Little People of the Shady Forest and the Sunny Meadow to read and write, you will have your hands full with the children. Be very careful, my dear, for they haven't yet learned to fly!"

"Don't worry," answered Mrs. Crow, "you have troubles enough with the schoolhouse full of children. I'll take good care that ours come to no harm."

Professor Jim Crow had been gone only a

few minutes when who should call but Grandmother Magpie.

"Good morning," she said, perching on a branch near at hand so as to look into the nestful of little crows.

"I'm dreadfully busy," answered Mrs. Crow. "Now that the Professor is teaching school, I have all the care of the children. It's no easy matter, for each little crow thinks he knows how to fly."

"Well, perhaps he does!" said Grandmother Magpie. "If you don't let them try how are they ever going to learn?"

"They are not old enough," replied Mrs. Crow.

"Not old enough?" repeated that meddlesome old lady bird. "Stuff and nonsense! Of course they are!" Then off she flew, leaving Mrs. Crow dreadfully upset and the little crows very discontented.

After making sure that Grandmother Magpie was out of sight, Mrs. Crow flew over to the Sunny Meadow for worms for her hungry children, but first she told them to be careful not to fall out of the nest while she was gone.

"Botheration!" said little Jimmy Crow after a few minutes. "Every word Grandmother Magpie says is true. We are kept like prisoners in this old nest. I'm going to fly!"

"Oh, don't!" cried all his brothers and sisters. "You can't fly even across the Shady Forest Path."

"Well, then, I can walk," said the naughty little crow, and he hopped out of the nest and fluttered down to the ground.

But, Oh dear me! Just then along came

the Farmer's Boy. In a twinkling, he
caught poor Jimmy Crow and cut off the
tips of his wing feathers with a big jack-
knife.

"Now, my little black beauty, you won't
fly far," he laughed, and turned his steps
toward the Old Farm.

> "So, you're caught, Jimmy Crow!"
>   Sang gay Billy Breeze,
> Playing hide-and-go-seek
>   'Mid the tall forest trees.

> "Don't you wish you'd obeyed
>   What your kind mother said?
> But, no, you were stubborn,
>   And had a swelled head."

A PRISONER

PRETTY soon along came Little Jack Rabbit on his way home from school. Everybody in the Shady Forest knew Little Jack Rabbit. From his nest in the Tall Pine Tree Jimmy Crow had often seen him hopping by with the Squirrel Brothers.

How he wished now he had never left the dear old nest. Here he was, a prisoner, and there was the little rabbit, free and happy, hopping home from school.

He tried to flutter out of the Farmer Boy's hand, but he was only held the tighter, so he lay perfectly still and wondered miserably what his mother would say when she came home and heard that he had disobeyed.

By and by the Farmer's Boy opened the gate to the Farmyard and walked over to the Big Red Barn. Pretty soon he found an old birdcage, in which he put poor Jimmy Crow. Then he hung it up on the little front porch of the Old Farm House.

"What have you got there," asked the Kind Farmer when he came home for supper, "a young crow?"

"Yep," answered the Farmer's Boy. "I picked him up in the woods; he was tryin' to fly."

It was very lonely on the little front porch after Mr. Merry Sun had gone to bed. Jimmy Crow huddled in one corner and watched Mrs. Moon climb over the hilltop.

He heard Granddaddy Bullfrog singing
in the Duck Pond, and the splash of the
millwheel as it turned slowly over and over.
How he wished he had obeyed his mother
and was safe at home, listening to his father
tell the school news, and who was late, and
who knew his lesson best.

By and by the Old Grandfather Clock in
the Farm House struck ten and the lights
went out. If it hadn't been for Mrs. Moon
it would have been pitch dark.

Suddenly, he heard a familiar hoot, and
the next minute dear Old Parson Owl fluttered up to the cage.

It didn't take him long to find the handle
on the little door, which he opened softly.

"Jump out!" he whispered. "Hop after
me as fast as you can. I'll fly low down so
you won't lose sight of me."

"Am I dreaming?" thought the poor little crow, as he fluttered down to the ground and hopped after Old Parson Owl toward the Shady Forest. "If I am, I hope I'll wake up in Mother's nest!"

HOME AGAIN

It was very late when they reached the Tall Pine Tree. The good Professor was sound asleep after a hard day's work in the Shady Forest Schoolhouse and a long search for his little lost crow. He had hunted for him until it grew so dark that he had been forced to give it up.

But Mrs. Crow was wide awake and the little crows were crying softly over their little lost brother. Disobedience makes others unhappy as well as the one who disobeys.

All of a sudden Mrs. Crow heard the gentle flap of wings, and looking over the

edge of the nest, she saw Old Parson Owl
in the dim moonlight. The next moment
the sight of little Jimmy Crow hopping
after him made her heart go pitter-patter.

"Here's our little boy!" she cried, flutter-
ing down to the ground, while all the little
crow brothers and sisters looked over the
edge of the nest, and Professor Jim Crow
woke up with a start.

But, dear me! Didn't they have a dreadful time getting the little crow up in the
tree. You see, he could only flutter now
that his wings had been clipped, and if Old
Parson Owl hadn't carried him on his
broad back, I doubt if Jimmy Crow ever
would have reached the nest.

By this time Mrs. Moon had crossed
over the sky, and Mr. Merry Sun was getting out of bed in the gold and purple East.

The Shady Forest was beginning to awake. The birds were chirping to one another, and the Little Four-footed People were racing up and down the trees and scampering over the ground.

Parson Owl waited to see that everything was all right, and then, turning to Professor Jim Crow, said:

"If Little Jack Rabbit hadn't come to tell me that the Farmer's Boy had stolen Jimmy Crow, your little son would still be in the cage on the farmhouse porch."

"My dear Parson," said Professor Jim Crow gratefully, "I shall never forget what you and Little Jack Rabbit have done."

"Don't mention it," said the kind old Parson, hurrying back to the Big Oak Tree before the light grew too strong for his big round eyes.

Oh, children, never disobey,
And never break a rule,
And never tell what is untrue,
Nor run away from school.

Perhaps if all the little boys and girls who read this story will learn this verse, it will keep them out of trouble. If Jimmy Crow had, maybe he never would have disobeyed his mother.

THE STOLEN EGGS

MR. MERRY SUN was up bright and early. He shone on the Sunny Meadow and lighted up the dark places in the Shady Forest.

He even poked a sunbeam in the eye of Parson Owl, who winked and blinked and turned the other way.

Soon everybody was wide awake, for the Little People of the Shady Forest and the Sunny Meadow are always up with Mr. Merry Sun.

Little Jack Rabbit, looking out of the Old Bramble Patch, wondered who was bending over the tall grass in the corner of the Old Rail Fence. Shading his eyes with his right paw, he looked again. Yes, it was the Farmer's Boy. Pretty soon he stood up straight, holding his hat carefully in his hand. Then he turned with a whistle and walked home.

"I wonder what he's been up to?" thought Little Jack Rabbit, and, being a curious little bunny, he hopped over to find out. Carefully peeping through the tall grass he saw a nice round nest, but it was empty. Only a gray speckled feather was left.

"He's stolen the eggs!" cried the little rabbit. "He's just mean enough to steal eggs!"

Just then Henny Penny came across the Sunny Meadow. She was a very pretty gray speckled hen and lived in a little house

"Did You Steal My Egg's?" Cried Henny Penny.

Little Jack Rabbit's Adventures.   *Page* 43

by the Big Red Barn. But instead of laying her nice white eggs in the comfortable
nests in the Henhouse, she came all the
way over to the Old Rail Fence Corner.

But Little Jack Rabbit didn't know that.
He didn't know whose nest it was until
Henny Penny cried distractedly, "Who has
stolen my eggs? Did you, Little Jack Rabbit?"

"Is it your nest?" he gasped, so startled
that he asked a question instead of answer-
ing one.

"Of course it's mine," replied Henny
Penny, looking at him as if she meant to
peck his little pink eyes right out of his
head. "But answer my question. Did you
take my eggs?"

"Of course not," said the little rabbit.
"I saw the hired boy leave here a few min-

utes ago with his hat in his hands. Maybe
he took them."

"Cock-a-doodle-do,
What can I do for you?"

asked a beautiful big rooster, all of a sudden, just like that.

"O Cocky Doodle!" cried Henny Penny,
"my nest has been robbed. Let's tell the
Kind Farmer that the hired boy has stolen
my eggs."

AT THE FARM

"ALL right, come along," said Cocky Doodle, and he started back for the Old Farm, followed by Henny Penny and the little bunny.

"Where are you going?" called out Mrs. Rabbit from the Old Bramble Patch.

"I'm going over to the Old Farm with Henny Penny and Cocky Doodle," answered her little bunny boy.

"You'd better be careful," said his mother, "the farmer might catch you."

"I don't think so, Mrs. Rabbit," said Cocky Doodle; "he's a very kind farmer." Mrs. Rabbit smiled, as if she only half believed the little rooster. Then she turned to her little rabbit boy and said, "Keep a bright lookout, and don't forget you're only a small bunny."

After that away went the three little people, Cocky Doodle, with his bright red comb, and Henny Penny in her pretty gray speckled feathers, and Little Jack Rabbit, in his fur waistcoat, white as the big clouds that chased Mr. Merry Sun over the bright blue sky.

"Who is this little bunny?" asked Turkey Tim when they all came to the Farm Yard.

"Don't you know?" answered Henny Penny. "Why, he's the little rabbit who colors the Easter Eggs!"

"What!" cried a big fat goose.

"This is Little Jack Rabbit," said Cocky Doodle.

"Pleased to meet you," said Goosey Lucy. "Do you paint goose eggs, too?" But before the little bunny could say yes or no, the Kind Farmer himself came out of the house.

"Why, look who's here," he said with a smile. And such a kind smile that Little Jack Rabbit wasn't the least bit afraid.

"He saw the hired boy steal the eggs from my nest in the corner of the Old Rail Fence," cried Henny Penny.

"Ha, ha!" laughed the Kind Farmer. "So that's where you've been laying your eggs, is it, Miss Henny Penny?"

'Cock-a-doodle-do,
She only laid a few.
But after this she'll lay the rest
Within the little wooden nest

> You hung upon the Henhouse wall,
> And tell you with her cackle-call,"

said the little rooster, for Henny Penny was
too ashamed to speak.

Then the Weathercock whirled around
on his big toe and, pointing at the little hen,
shouted through his tin megaphone:

> "Why don't you stay at home and lay,
> And not go calling every day?
> I never leave my perch up here
> No matter what the atmosphere."

COLORED EGGS

"I OFTEN wondered why she went across the Sunny Meadow every day," said Ducky Waddles. "It's too long a walk for me!"

"Yes, you wabble too much!" said Henny Penny.

"That's because I've little thin pieces of skin between my toes," answered Ducky Waddles. "My feet are too wide and flat for walking, but they make splendid paddles."

"Come, come," interrupted the Kind Farmer. "Henny Penny hasn't explained why she goes over to the Sunny Meadow to lay her eggs instead of in the nice nests in the Henhouse."

"Because I wanted Little Jack Rabbit to color them for Easter," she answered. "I thought if I laid them near the Old Bramble Patch it would be easier for him."

"Oh, that's the reason?" said the Kind Farmer. "And pray, Mr. Jack Rabbit, how do you color the eggs?"

Oh, dear me! Wasn't the little rabbit embarrassed! He wasn't sure but what he'd better hop back to the Old Bramble Patch. Perhaps, too, he was a little bit afraid of the big Kind Farmer.

"I never colored any eggs," answered the little rabbit in a low voice, "but I've often helped mother color them. She takes a big red rose and rubs it over an egg until it turns red. With a buttercup she makes a

yellow one. From the violets by the Bubbling Brook she gets a beautiful purple
color, and from the wild roses a lovely pink
tint. Just every-day grass gives a dandy
green color."

"Ha, ha," laughed the big Kind Farmer,
"so that's what the rabbits do on Easter, is
it?" and he turned away and went into the
Big Red Barn to feed the horses.

"I guess it's time for me to be going,"
said Little Jack Rabbit. "Mother may
worry if I stay away too long!"

"What's your hurry?" said Ducky Waddles.

"Goodby," said Henny Penny.

"Come again," said Cocky Doodle.

"Come very soon," said Turkey Tim.

"Call tomorrow," cried Goosey Lucy.

But the little rabbit was out of hearing by
this time, and just as Mr. Merry Sun went
down behind the West Hill, he hopped into
the Old Bramble Patch.

"Come, wash your hands; supper is
ready," said Mrs. Rabbit, as she took the
carrot muffins out of the oven and dished
the stewed lollypops.

HENNY PENNY'S MISTAKE

THERE was great excitement at the Old Barn Yard. A big mistake had been made. Whose fault it was no one could tell; but the fact was that Henny Penny had hatched out a brood of ducklings.

At first nobody thought anything was wrong, except that, perhaps, her little brood had very large bills and feet, much larger than those of any little chicks at the farm.

But one day when the whole brood waddled off down to the Old Duck Pond and jumped in everybody knew that Henny Penny had little ducks and not little chickens.

53

Poor little Henny Penny! She stood upon the bank and clucked and clucked to them to come back.

"You'll be drowned, my darlings!" she cried. But the little ducks threw out their great brown feet as cleverly as if they had taken swimming lessons all their lives and sailed off on the Old Duck Pond, away, away among the ferns, under the pink azaleas, through reeds and rushes and arrowheads and pickerel weed, the happiest ducks that ever were born. And soon they were quite out of sight.

Poor little Henny Penny. She didn't know how to swim, so she sat down on the bank and waited for her little ducks to come back. Now and then she wiped her eyes on her downy breast feathers.

"Don't cry," said Cocky Doodle kindly.

"Don't worry," said Rosy Comb. "Your children seem to know how to swim as well as Ducky Waddles."

Just then across the Old Duck Pond came a chorus of quacks, and at a distance was seen the little brood swimming home, their feathers gleaming in green and gold.

"Such a splendid time we've had," they all cried as they waddled up the bank. "And we know now how to get our own living, for there are lots of little fish and flies out there on the Old Duck Pond. We can take care of ourselves, so don't worry any more about us, Mother Henny Penny."

"They are little ducks, not chickens," said Ducky Waddles.

"Are you sure?" asked Henny Penny

tearfully, wiping her eyes with a tiny yellow handkerchief.

"Of course I am," replied Ducky Waddles. "Don't I know a duck's foot when I see it?"

"Dear, Oh dear!" sighed the poor little hen, "there has been a dreadful mistake!"

But whose mistake it was no one could tell, for the Kind Farmer never confessed that he put duck eggs in Henny Penny's nest.

THE DAM

THE Bubbling Brook was slowly drying up. Everyone on the Sunny Meadow was worried, and the little people who lived in the water were even more worried.

It was just like having one's house pulled down while living in it. You see, as the water became more shallow there were places in the little brook that were hardly covered with water, and it was only in the deep holes that the fish and crabs could swim at all.

And the cause of all this was Busy Beaver. Yes, sir. Busy Beaver was building a dam across the Bubbling Brook.

Somehow he knew that winter was coming, when it would be all frozen over. But he knew that if he built a dam across it, a little pond would form where the water would be too deep to freeze clear down to the bottom.

"I'll leave a little opening in the dam to let the water run out when it gets high enough," said Busy Beaver to himself as he laid mud and stones on top of a log.

If the Little People of the Sunny Meadow had only heard him they wouldn't have been so worried. Little Jack Rabbit did, though, as he came hopping down the Shady Forest Path.

"Good morning," said the little bunny.

Busy Beaver looked up from his work. He had almost finished a mighty good job. First, he had cut down a tree, and then

sawed it with his sharp teeth into logs.
These he had rolled into the water, weight-
ing them down with stones and mud until
gradually he had built up a splendid dam
from the bottom of the pond.

"It's almost finished," said Busy Beaver.
"It took me quite a long time, for sometimes the logs would bob up and drift away,
and I'd have to begin all over again. But
I kept at it, and now I've got a nice dam
to hold back the water."

"Why do you want deep water?" asked
the little rabbit.

"Come over here and I'll show you," answered Busy Beaver, leading Little Jack
Rabbit around to the end of the dam nearest
the Shady Forest. "There, you see my
house. Now the water must be deep enough
so that when it freezes my front door will

always be below the ice. Otherwise I wouldn't be able to swim in and out."

"How soon will the Bubbling Brook start running again?" asked the little bunny.

"Pretty soon—maybe tonight," answered Busy Beaver.

"Hurrah! I'll tell my friend the little Fresh Water Crab!" and away hopped the little rabbit to the Sunny Meadow.

GOOD NEWS

ALREADY the water was beginning to trickle over the pebbly bottom of the Bubbling Brook.

All of a sudden a voice overhead shouted, "Good morning!" and there sat Chatterbox, the Red Squirrel, in the Big Walnut Tree. "Why are you in such a hurry?"

"I must tell all my friends in the Sunny Meadow the good news," replied the little rabbit. "I can't wait a minute."

"I'll go with you," said Chatterbox, running down the tree. "Tell me, what's the news?"

"The Bubbling Brook will be running

again tonight," answered the little bunny,
and he explained all about Busy Beaver's
dam.

"Well, I declare," exclaimed Chatterbox,
"Busy Beaver has a lot of nerve to stop the
water running in the Bubbling Brook. He
doesn't own the water rights. The Bubbling Brook belongs to everyone alike."

"So it does," answered Little Jack Rabbit,
"but Busy Beaver has to look out for himself. If he doesn't build a dam his little
house will be frozen up this winter."

Just then the water rose almost to the
ferns that grew on the edge of the Bubbling
Brook. "Everything's all right now," said
the little rabbit, "I won't bother to go over
to the Sunny Meadow. The fishes and the
little fresh water crabs will learn the news

before I can get there," and he sat down to talk things over with Chatterbox.

"You just ought to see Busy Beaver use his tail as a trowel to lay on the mud," said the little rabbit, who couldn't keep from talking about what he had just seen. "He carries the mud and stones between his chin and forepaws and knows just how to put them in the cracks between the logs to keep back the water."

"Well, we all must prepare for the long, cold winter," said Chatterbox. "Brother Tip Top and I have been gathering nuts for many a day and have our storehouse nearly full."

While the Autumn days are here
Make things snug for Winter drear;
Storehouse filled with everything
To last until again it's Spring.

A PERPLEXED LITTLE RABBIT

"GOODNESS gracious me!" exclaimed Little Jack Rabbit, all of a sudden, "the Clover Patch is all dried up. What shall I do when winter comes?"

"Hunt for old turnips and carrots in the field," laughed Chatterbox.

"I think I'll leave you," answered Little Jack Rabbit thoughtfully, "I'm beginning to worry about what's going to happen to me," and away he hopped, leaving the little red squirrel sitting beneath his tree.

" 'Most everybody I know," thought the little rabbit as he hopped along, "curls up and goes to sleep for the winter. I wonder

if I could? I'm going home to ask
Mother."

But Mrs. Rabbit was too busy putting up
carrot jelly to answer questions. "Don't
bother me," she said, "I haven't got a minute
to spare." So the only thing for the little
bunny to do was to go to somebody else.

The very first person he met was Hedgy
Hedgehog. He was just coming out of his
hole, which he had been busily lining with
grass and dry leaves, some of which were
still sticking to his spikes, for he hadn't
had time to brush himself.

"What are you doing?" asked the little
bunny.

"Getting ready for winter. I've fixed up
my place nice and warm, and when the cold
weather comes I'll creep in and sleep till
Spring."

"What do you eat?" asked Little Jack
Rabbit, who could eat all the time, and
sometimes oftener, like all rabbits.

"Don't eat—can't eat when you're asleep,
you know."

"Gracious me!" exclaimed the little
bunny, "that would never do for me!" and
he hopped away.

By and by he came to the Old Duck Pond.
There sat Granddaddy Bullfrog on a log,
winking and blinking in the light of Mr.
Merry Sun.

"Granddaddy Bullfrog, what do you do
when winter comes?"

"Why, bless you, my little bunny,"
answered the old gentleman frog, "I go
to sleep in the mud at the bottom of
the pond."

"Oh, dear, I can't do that!" sighed the little rabbit.

"Of course not," laughed Granddaddy Bullfrog. "Do what your mother says, and stop worrying!"

THE TURNIP

"WELL, I guess Granddaddy Bullfrog is right," thought Little Jack Rabbit, as he hopped back home to the Old Bramble Patch. "What's the use of worrying about winter? I'll take Granddaddy Bullfrog's advice and leave it all to Mother."

After that he felt much better. Pretty soon he saw Timmy Meadowmouse looking out of his little round house of grass, no larger than a cricket ball, which was fastened to three or four stiff stalks of grass about a foot above the ground.

"Good morning. Do you know, I've been dreadfully worried about winter; but

now I'm going to take Granddaddy Bullfrog's advice and leave it all to mother."

You see, this little rabbit just couldn't
stop talking about his troubles, although he
was going to leave them all to mother!

"There! She's waving to you from the
Old Bramble Patch," cried Timmy Meadowmouse. Away went the little bunny
without another word and in less than five
hundred hops he was home.

"Hop over to the field and bring me a
turnip. Your father will be home for lunch
in a few minutes," said Mrs. Rabbit.

Little Jack Rabbit hopped through the
Old Rail Fence, across the road and into
the field where the Old Scarecrow flapped
his arms every time Billy Breeze whistled
through the cornstalks. But the Old
Clothes Man couldn't frighten the little

bunny. Oh, my no! It took more than that, although he was a scary little chap. You see, he knew all about the Old Scarecrow, for he had watched the Kind Farmer put him up in the early Spring.

Picking up a nice looking turnip, he turned about and started back again. But, Oh dear me! All of a sudden out from behind a cornstack jumped the Farmer's Boy.

The little rabbit didn't stop to say sorry to have met you. No siree. He hopped away as fast as he could, but not fast enough. Before he had gone maybe thirteen hops a stone hit his left hind leg.

"Ha, ha!" yelled the Farmer's Boy. "Wait till I hit you again, Mr. Cottontail. But he didn't, for the little rabbit went faster on three legs than he had on four, and

the next minute popped safely into the dear
Old Bramble Patch.

"Where's the turnip?" asked Mrs. Rabbit.

"Goodness me! I guess that's what the
Farmer's Boy hit me with," answered the
little bunny.

THE BONFIRE

EVERYBODY in the Shady Forest was having a dreadful time. Old Parson Owl was nearly coughing his head off, Professor Jim Crow's voice was so hoarse his scholars could hardly understand him, and Little Jack Rabbit's eyes looked as if he had been crying for a week.

The reason for all this was that the smoke from the Farmer Boy's big bonfire had drifted into the forest until every chink and corner was filled.

At first no one knew what was the matter. Of course the air smelled queer and made one's eyes smart. But after a while when the smoke grew so thick that it seemed like night-time and Mr. Merry Sun couldn't be seen at all, the Forest Folk thought it time to hold a meeting to consider what was best to do. They all decided to ask Billy Breeze to help them, and you can imagine how grateful they were when he agreed to blow the smoke out of the Shady Forest. Before Mr. Merry Sun went down behind the hills that night Billy Breeze had cleared the smoke away and everything was clean and sweet again.

Now, before all this had taken place, a handful of burning leaves had drifted along the Old Rail Fence, setting fire to the long, dry grass, and in a short time there was quite a fire close to the Old Bramble Patch.

It didn't take Little Jack Rabbit long to

borrow some sweet potatoes from his
mother, and while he was roasting them
Chippy Chipmunk climbed through the
fence with a bagful of chestnuts.

Pretty soon along came Jimmy Crow,
and when he saw what was going on, he
was mighty anxious to have some fun, too.
So off he went to get some bittersweet berries, for he likes them much better than
sweet potatoes.

After a while Mrs. Rabbit came out to
see whether they were up to any mischief.
She was worried for fear they might burn
up the Old Rail Fence or set fire to the Old
Bramble Patch. But no, nothing was
wrong. All three were quietly sitting
around a small fire, the little rabbit peeling
a hot sweet potato, the little chipmunk shell-
ing a smoking hot chestnut and the little

crow picking out the nice browned bitter-sweet berries.

"Well, well!" exclaimed the lady rabbit with a sigh of relief, "I expected to see the Old Rail Fence in ashes and the dear Old Bramble Patch in flames."

MRS. COW

"TING-A-LING! ting-a-ling!" went Mrs. Cow's bell. Mrs. Cow seemed mighty anxious to get away from somebody. Yes, sir! she kept right on running, although every now and then she'd turn her head to look behind her.

By and by Little Jack Rabbit came hopping over the top of the hill with a tin pail in his paw. But, goodness me! Mrs. Cow didn't have to run away from him. No indeed. He wasn't going to milk her. He didn't have a milk pail at all, but a little dinner pail, and Mrs. Cow was mistaken and had run away for nothing.

The truth of the matter was that the little

rabbit was going berrying down in the
Cranberry Marsh on the other side of the
Old Duck Pond, but of course Mrs. Cow
didn't know that.

But she did know it wasn't time to be
milked, and, anyway, she wasn't going to
have anybody milk her but the Kind
Farmer.

"Mrs. Cow! Mrs. Cow!" cried the little
rabbit, "I'm going cranberrying, not milk-
ing. Don't run away!"

"Honest Injun?" said Mrs. Cow, halting
at the Bubbling Brook. "Cross your
heart?"

"Yes, cross my heart," answered the little rabbit.

"Well, I'm glad to hear you say so," replied Mrs. Cow. "I might have sprained my
ankle jumping over the Bubbling Brook."

Then she trotted along by the little rabbit's side.

"How's your Ma these days?" she asked in a little while.

"She's going to make cranberry jelly when I get back," replied the little rabbit. "Father's very fond of it. How's Mr. Bull?"

"He's very well," answered Mrs. Cow. "He was up when Cocky Doodle sang his Sun Song this morning."

"So was I," laughed the little rabbit. "Mother says Cocky Doodle is better than an alarm clock, for you don't have to wind him."

Just then they came to the end of the meadow, so the little rabbit hopped through the fence and down to the Cranberry Patch to fill his pail with the bright red berries.

THE SUGAR-COATED CARROT

ALL of a sudden, just like that, he saw something shining in the grass. And what do you think it was? You'll never guess, so I'll tell you right away. A sugar-coated carrot. But before he could put it in his pocket along came little Katie Cottontail, swinging her sunbonnet in her paw.

"Wiggle your ear and shut your eye,
Twinkle your nose and say 'Oh my!'"

shouted Little Jack Rabbit, "and I'll give you something to make you laugh."

"What is it?" asked little Katie Cottontail, but just the same she didn't wait for an answer, but closed her eyes and twinkled her nose up and down, and then sideways.

But, Oh dear me. Just then the little rabbit dropped the sugar-coated carrot and couldn't find it. He hunted high and low, and so did little Katie Cottontail, but the candy carrot was gone. Yes, sir. It certainly was. And I'll tell you where it went. Into a little hole in the ground where a snake had his home.

"Well, we'll make some cranberry juice soda when we get home," said Little Jack Rabbit, and off they hopped to the Cranberry Patch. In a little while he had filled his pail and Katie Cottontail her apron, and then they started for home.

"I must be careful not to squash 'em, or

Mother'll give me a scolding," she said, as they climbed up the bank where the railroad track cut through. But, Oh dear me! Just as they were about to hop through the Old Rail Fence, along came a train.

"Ding, dong!" went the bell. "Toot-toot-toot!" shrieked the whistle. Poor little Katie Cottontail gave a shiver and dropped her apron. Then clipperty-clip, lipperty-lip she went up the Cow Path to the Old Brush Heap on the hillside.

Mrs. Cow looked up and, seeing the little bunny girl hopping home all out of breath, thought something must be the matter and ran back to the Big Red Barn. The bell on her collar didn't make nearly as much noise as the one on the locomotive, but it made her hurry, just the same.

"Goodness me! What scary things girls are!" said the little rabbit. "Mrs. Cow's ten times as big as Katie Cottontail, but she's just as scary."

After picking up the cranberries which the little frightened girl rabbit had spilled from her apron, the bunny boy hopped home to the Old Bramble Patch.

His mother was standing in the kitchen doorway, her right paw shading her eyes as she looked anxiously over the Sunny Meadow.

Katie Cottontail Went Clippety-Clap Up the Path.

Little Jack Rabbit's Adventures. *Page* 81

BAD LUCK

"GOODNESS me! I'm dreadfully worried," cried Mrs. Rabbit, "I just saw the Kind Farmer's Black Cat cross the path from right to left, and that means bad luck, you know."

"I guess he's hunting for little Timmy Meadowmouse," answered Little Jack Rabbit. "It will be bad luck for Timmy to be caught."

"Why don't you run over and tell him," said Mrs. Rabbit. "Black Cat may be hiding near his house. You'd better hurry."

So away hopped the little rabbit to find Timmy Meadowmouse, who lived in a little round house made of twisted grass on the Sunny Meadow. Pretty soon he saw the little meadowmouse peeking out of his front door.

"Oh, it's you, is it, Little Jack Rabbit," he said with a sigh of relief, "I thought I heard some one creeping around my house. But if it was you, it's all right."

"Maybe it isn't all right," answered the little rabbit, and he told how his mother had seen Black Cat cross the path from right to left. "And that means bad luck, you know."

"If he crosses your path from left to right, what does that mean?" asked the little mea-dowmouse.

"Good luck," answered Little Jack Rabbit.

"I don't know," said Timmy Meadow-mouse with a shiver, "if he saw me first, it

would be bad luck no matter which way he
crossed the path."

Just then Little Jack Rabbit saw something move in the tall grass. "Look out,"
he shouted.

Into his house popped Timmy Meadowmouse, and none too soon, for Black Cat
landed on the very spot where he had stood
talking to the little rabbit.

"So it was you who warned Timmy
Meadowmouse, was it?" he hissed, hump-
ing up his back and waving his long tail
back and forth. Oh my, but he looked
ugly.

"Yes, it was I," answered Little Jack
Rabbit bravely, and then he did what his
mother had taught him to do when in a
tight place. He suddenly turned his back
on Black Cat and struck out with his strong

hind legs. Thump! they went against
Black Cat's ribs, knocking him over.   Then
away hopped the little rabbit back to the
Old Bramble Patch.

> If you do what mother says
>   You'll grow tall and strong.
> On your lips a happy smile,
>   In your heart a song—
> If you do what mother says
>   You will not go wrong.

LITTLE JACK RABBIT STUBS HIS TOE

Cocky Doodle stood by the Big Red Barn and clapped his wings. Then digging his feet well into the ground, he began his morning cock-a-doodle-do.

Mr. Merry Sun lifted his head from his crimson pillows and looked over the misty hilltop.

"Time for me to get up," he yawned. "Cocky Doodle is calling."

Teddy Turtle crawled along the Old Cow Path to the Old Duck Pond. He didn't see Little Jack Rabbit hopping over the grass. Teddy is so slow that he never thinks any one can go faster. So it was only when the little rabbit stubbed his toe on the little turtle's hard shell house that he woke up. Of course he wasn't really asleep, but he might just as well have been.

"You ought to know better than to go to sleep right in the Old Cow Path," said the little bunny, rubbing his toe. "Why don't you keep your head out to see where you're going if you walk in your sleep?"

"I pulled my head inside my shell when you hit me, as all well-trained turtles do in time of danger," answered Teddy Turtle.

"Goodness, I wouldn't be afraid of anything if I had a strong shell house like yours to creep into."

"Well, I'm not afraid of anybody except the Miller's Boy," said Teddy Turtle.

"But when he turns me over on my back I'm helpless."

"Where are you going?" asked the little rabbit.

"Down to the Old Duck Pond. I'm going to sleep in the soft mud for the winter," answered Teddy Turtle.

"Well, goodby," said the little rabbit, hopping off to the Old Farm Yard.

"Cock-a-doodle-do," sang Cocky Doodle. "I hope everybody is awake. There comes Mr. Merry Sun up the sky. Cock-a-doodle-do. Everybody gets up when I call. Don't you hear Billy Breeze singing over the Sunny Meadow? I wake the Little People of the Shady Forest and the Sunny Meadow every morning. Cock-a-doodle-do."

Yes, sir. This little rooster was better than an alarm clock, for you didn't have to wind him. He crowed every morning his cheerful song to help the old world wag along.

MUD TURTLE TOWN

THE Mud Turtles were having a fine time on the banks of the Old Duck Pond. What is more fun I should like to know than making mud pies and forts, and these little turtles had been busy for several days until they had built a mud city, with bridges and houses, towers and castles.

Goodness me! It was muddy, and the Farmyard Folk were all complaining, except Ducky Waddles. He just loved mud, and found it great fun waddling over the mud bridges. And if they broke down, he didn't mind a muddy splashing! No, indeed he didn't. So, of course, he and the Mud Turtles were great friends.

One day Mr. Merry Sun, seeing how things were going on, said to himself: "I guess I'll dry up all the Turtle Mud Houses." So he set to work, shining down from the bright blue sky, and before evening the mud palaces and castles were hard as bricks.

"Hurrah!" he said, just before he went to sleep on the crimson pillows of the West, "I've finished Mud Turtle Town!"

Of course, all this was more or less of an accident, for the Mud Turtles hadn't asked Mr. Merry Sun to help them. But when they saw what he had done, they were delighted, and at once sent out invitations to all the Barnyard Folk to spend a week in Turtle Town.

Cocky Doodle and Henny Penny accepted at once; so did Goosey Lucy; and as soon as they had packed their things, they set out for the Old Duck Pond.

"I don't think I shall lay an egg while I'm there," said Henny Penny—"I'm not used to Mud Nests."

"Suit yourself," said Cocky Doodle.

"Henny Penny is right," said Goosey Lucy. "It will be a little vacation for us. I, for one, shall be glad to forget all about home duties."

Just then there was a great flapping of wings and Ducky Waddles came wabbling after them. "Why don't you wait for a fellow," he panted. "I'm all out of breath trying to catch up to you. I almost had to fly."

As they crossed the Old Cow Path they met Little Jack Rabbit hopping home to the Old Bramble Patch.

"We're going to make a visit in Turtle Town," said Henny Penny. "Why don't you come, too?"

"Haven't time," answered the little bunny. "Mother sent me over to Cousin Cottontail for lollypop frosting. She must have it in time to cover the carrot cake for supper."

BOBBY TAIL

MR. JOHN RABBIT had been a great jumper in his youth, and Little Jack Rabbit wished to learn to jump as far as his father, and even farther.

So every day he practiced jumping in the Sweet Clover Field near the Old Rail Fence until by and by he could jump over the second rail.

"Pretty good," said Mr. Rabbit. "Don't believe I did any better when I was your age. How is Bobby Tail getting along?"

Now Little Jack Rabbit's brother was called Bobby Tail, because his tail was so short. Yes, siree, it was so short that it

looked exactly like a white powder puff.
And his eyes were just like little pink beads.
But they weren't any pinker than his nose.

But, I'm sorry to say, there was something wrong with Bobby Tail. He was too
lazy for anything. That was what was the
matter with him. He didn't want to learn
to jump—he'd rather spend his time eating
clover tops. By and by he grew to be dreadfully fat.

And a fat bunny can't run fast nor jump
far. Bobby Tail found this to be true when
one day Sic'em, the Farmer's Dog, chased
him across the Sunny Meadow.

The Bunny Brothers had hopped down
to the Old Duck Pond to see Granddaddy
Bullfrog, when all of a sudden Sic'em saw
them. Goodness me! What a chase he gave
them! Over the Sunny Meadow, through

the Shady Forest, and along the Old Rail
Fence! At first Bobby Tail was able to
keep up with brother, but after a while he
fell behind.

"Hurry up!" shouted Little Jack Rabbit.
But, Oh dear me! Bobby Tail was so fat
and so short of breath that he couldn't.
Closer and closer came Sic'em till the little
bunny could almost feel his hot breath.

"If I ever get back to the Old Bramble
Patch," he thought, "I'll practice running
and jumping every day in the week."

Just then, he reached the Old Rail Fence.
Another jump landed him in the dear Old
Bramble Patch, leaving Sic'em barking
and growling outside the prickly bushes.

"You've had a narrow escape," said Mr.
Rabbit, looking up over his evening paper,
"I hope it will teach you a lesson!"

And it did. The very next day Bobby
Tail practiced jumping with Little Jack
Rabbit, and kept it up until he became al-
most as good a jumper as his brother.

But Old Sic'em never knew how this
came to pass. He was too busy keeping
watch over the Old Farmyard to bother his
head about Bobby Tail, for Danny Fox,
who was always prowling around, hunting
for a stray chicken, kept the old dog for-
ever on the lookout.

SUNSHINE

"WHERE did you get your red coat?" asked Little Jack Rabbit, looking up from the Old Bramble Patch.

"Oh, that's my secret," answered Red Bird from the Old Rail Fence. "There's been a legend in our family about it ever since the Flood."

"You don't say so," exclaimed the little rabbit.

"You've heard of the Great Flood, I suppose, that happened hundreds and hundreds of years ago?"

Little Jack Rabbit nodded. "I hope we don't get another to wash away the Old Bramble Patch."

"Well," continued Red Bird, "the legend is that one day, after it had been raining ever so long, when there was nothing but water all around and everybody in the ark was feeling very miserable, Mother Noah wrung her hands and said, 'Oh, dear! We'll all be lost. We'll never get ashore!'

"Just then my ancestor began to whistle, and the next minute a beam of sunshine broke through the clouds and settled upon him.

" 'My dear, we are reproved,' said Father Noah. 'The little bird has more courage than we have. Hear him whistle.'

"Then everybody turned to look at the brave little whistler. He was so embarrassed that he BLUSHED—we were gray before that time, they say—blushed so very deeply that our feathers have never lost their bright red from that day to this."

"Well, well," exclaimed the little rabbit. "When do you go away for the winter?"

"I'm not going away—I'm going to stay right here," answered Red Bird.

"You'll find it pretty breezy up there," said Little Jack Rabbit with a twinkle of his pink nose.

"Oh, I don't know. I've got on my double-breasted red coat."

"But what will you find to eat when the berries are all gone?" asked the little rabbit.

"I'll pick up crumbs at the Old Farm House," replied Red Bird cheerfully.

"You've got a sunshiny disposition," said Little Jack Rabbit admiringly. "I guess your ancestors handed down something be-

sides a red coat—some of that sunshine that
turned his feathers red must have crept into
his heart."

"I don't know," replied Red Bird.

"Maybe it doesn't make much difference
how you got it, as long as you keep it," said
the little bunny as he hopped back into the
Old Bramble Patch to tell his mother all
about it.

TURKEY TIM

Turkey Tim in his turban-colored comb strutted about the Old Farmyard, spreading his tail like a Japanese fan to the bright light that Mr. Merry Sun sent down from the Big Blue Sky.

"I wonder what makes Turkey Tim so proud?" asked Henny Penny.

Little Jack Rabbit wiggled his pink nose, but said nothing.

"Is it because the Kind Farmer is buying chestnuts for him from Chippy Chipmunk?"

Still the little rabbit made no reply.

"Please tell me," begged Henny Penny. "You can whisper in my ear."

"Turkey Tim thinks the Kind Farmer is fond of him, but that's not the reason," answered the little rabbit.

"What is the reason?" asked Henny Penny, who you see by this time was a very curious little hen.

"Turkey Tim wouldn't believe me if I told him," said the little rabbit.

"Wouldn't he?" exclaimed the little hen, her feathers ruffled with excitement and curiosity.

"It's a big secret," whispered the little bunny.

"Tell me quick," coaxed Henny Penny.

"Thanksgiving!" whispered Little Jack Rabbit. "Haven't you heard of chestnut-fed turkeys for Thanksgiving?"

"Do you mean they are going to kill Turkey Tim?" cried the little hen.

"I certainly do," answered the little rabbit. "But he's so proud he wouldn't believe me. Why, he thinks he's more wonderful than Cocky Doodle."

"Well, he isn't," said Henny Penny. "Cocky Doodle's the most wonderful of all the Feathered Folk, for he's the one who wakes up Mr. Merry Sun. Cocky Doodle is the cock-a-doodle-do clock of the whole wide world. Why, if it weren't for him Mr. Merry Sun might stay in bed all day."

Just then along came Turkey Tim, but he didn't look so proud when the little hen told him about Thanksgiving.

"Who told you?" he asked in a trembling voice.

"Little Jack Rabbit," answered Henny Penny, pointing to the truthful little bunny.

"I guess I'll make a visit in the Friendly Forest," said Turkey Tim in a low voice, and off he went as fast as his legs would take him.

But, Oh dear me! No sooner was he there than Billy Breeze began to sing:

> "Look out, look out for Danny Fox!
>   He sneaks about in his woolen socks,
>   You never can tell where he is at,
>   For he creeps around like a tip-toe cat."

PHOEBE PHEASANT

LITTLE Phoebe Pheasant's dew-wet feet hurried along the edge of the Sunny Meadow. Mr. Merry Sun hadn't been up long enough to dry the grass, for it was very early in the morning.

In some places the dew had turned to frost, but the little pheasant didn't mind that in the least, for she is a hardy bird, and not a bit afraid of cold weather.

The weather is about the only thing she isn't afraid of, for she is very timid. Although she sometimes went to the Old Farmyard for breakfast, at the slightest noise she would fly away.

As she hurried along through the dewy frost she caught sight of Little Jack Rabbit. And as he was the one person she wished to see that morning, it didn't take her long to reach the Old Bramble Patch.

"Good morning, Phoebe Pheasant," said the little bunny. "You seem in a hurry."

"Yes, I'm in a dreadful hurry to ask you something," replied the little pheasant.

"Well, what is it?" laughed the little bunny.

"You remember Turkey Tim left the Old Farmyard before Thanksgiving?"

"Of course I do," answered the little rabbit.

"He wants to know whether the Kind Farmer has been looking for him?" whispered Phoebe Pheasant. "He doesn't dare go back himself to find out."

"I should say not," answered the little
rabbit. "The Kind Farmer's dreadfully put
out. He had to go without his Thanksgiving turkey!"

"Then you think it would be dangerous
for Turkey Tim to go back to the Old
Farmyard?"

"Yes, just now," replied the little bunny.
"He'd better wait until everybody has for-
gotten Thanksgiving."

"It's dreadfully hard on him, all alone
in the Shady Forest," sighed the little pheasant. "He's not a Wild Turkey, you know."

"Never mind if he isn't," answered Little
Jack Rabbit. "He'll be a Roast Turkey if
he goes back now to the Old Farmyard."

THE SNOWBALL

BILLY BREEZE had kicked up an awful racket all night around the Old Briar Patch, but Little Jack Rabbit hadn't heard him. No, sir. The little bunny had been too sound asleep to hear anything, but when he looked out in the morning, goodness me! how he shivered.

The ground was all covered with a white mantle, but he didn't know it was snow. This was the first snow he had ever seen. It made everything look strange, and the ground was as smooth as Mrs. Rabbit's best linen tablecloth.

Pretty soon he hopped down to the Bub-

bling Brook, but it, too, had changed. It
was smooth, like glass So the little rabbit
leaned over the bank to listen, but just then
Billy Breeze made a dreadful racket and
whirled the snow about in great clouds. But
the little rabbit didn't care; he just kept
on listening, and by and by he heard the
Bubbling Brook singing softly:

> "Underneath the ice and snow
> Very gently still I flow
> Till I reach the Old Duck Pond
> And the ocean far beyond.

> "Billy Breeze may whistle loud
> Toss the snow up in a cloud,
> Underneath the ice and snow
> Very gently still I flow."

"Dear me," said the little rabbit to himself, "I never would know that this was the
Old Duck Pond if it weren't for the Old

Mill yonder. No wonder Granddaddy Bullfrog hid himself deep down in the mud before all this happened."

Yes, the whole earth seemed quiet and still. The mill wheel moved no more; great icicles hung from the paddles and long snowdrifts lay piled against the dam.

I don't know how long the little rabbit would have stood there wondering at the sudden change if something hadn't happened. Whiz! went a snowball past his ear. The Farmer's Boy leaned over and picked up some more snow. But the little rabbit didn't wait to see what sort of a snowball he would make this time. No, siree. He hopped back to the dear Old Bramble Patch as fast as he could.

THE NEW SLEIGH

THE Old Farm Yard was a very comfortable sort of a place. Little Jack Rabbit liked to go there, for all the Barnyard Folk were very nice to him, especially Henny Penny and Cocky Doodle, who always gave him some of their corn.

Then, too, it was great fun playing about the High Haystack. Here they all gathered after a snow storm, for the snow soon melted on the sunny side.

Another reason, too, why the little rabbit came so often was because many of his friends were tucked away for a long winter's nap.

Busy Beaver was safe in his little house under the ice in the Forest Pool. Squirrel Nutcracker and his family came out only on warm, sunshiny days. The rest of the time they spent sleeping in their warm little houses. As for Granddaddy Bullfrog, he never showed up—he was sound asleep in the soft mud at the bottom of the Old Duck Pond.

The little rabbit's mother had told him not to go too often to the Old Farm Yard for fear the Kind Farmer might not like it. "Henny Penny and Cocky Doodle are your friends," she told him, "but I'm not so sure about Mr. Farmer."

"Oh, he's all right, mother," answered the little rabbit. "He's very kind. He feeds all the Barn Yard Folk with such nice

"I'm So Tired of Polishing This Doorknob."

Little Jack Rabbit's Adventures.

Page 117

food. I'm sure he's very good and kind."

"Don't be too sure," answered the little rabbit's mother, with a knowing wag of her head.

One day when the little bunny hopped into the Old Farm Yard he heard Cocky Doodle say:

"It's a beautiful sleigh!" And just as Little Jack Rabbit was going to ask what he meant, the Kind Farmer came out of the Big Red Barn with Betsy, the Old Gray Mare, and hitched her up to a beautiful dark green sleigh.

"Git ap!" he said, snapping the whip over her back.

"Oh, Oh!" cried the little rabbit, "Maybe mother is right. I guess he's not such a kind farmer after all!" But of course the little bunny didn't know that the Kind Farmer hardly touched Old Betsy, although the whip made a loud crack and she threw out her heels and ran off at a great rate.

"Jingle bells, jingle bells,
  On the nice new sleigh.
  Oh what fun it is to run!"
Sang dear Old Betsy Gray.

DAILY DUTIES

It isn't always easy
  To do the things you must.
Some people if they stay at home
  Say they will surely rust.
But you will find the longer
  You live from day to day
That you must do the little things
  That daily come your way.

"OH, dear!" sighed Little Jack Rabbit one lovely spring morning, "I'm so tired of polishing this doorknob every day and every day. I wish it would drop off."

"Goodness me, little rabbit," said Grandmother Magpie, who just then happened along, "you are a disagreeable bunny boy

117

this morning." And the old lady magpie looked at him out of her little black eyes as much as to say: "I wish I had that bunny boy to bring up, I'd make him toe the mark."

And perhaps she would, and perhaps she wouldn't, for some people can bring up other people's children ever so much better than their own, or even themselves. Isn't that strange? Well, maybe it is and maybe it isn't.

"What are you saying to my little bunny boy?" asked Mrs. John Rabbit, putting her head out of the kitchen window and scowling at Grandmother Magpie.

"Oh, nothing much," said that meddlesome old lady bird.

"Well, you'd better not," said Mrs. Rabbit. "It's all you can do to gossip about

grown-up people's affairs." And then Mrs.
Rabbit shook her dusting rag up and down,
and maybe once sideways, and after that she
shut the window. So Grandmother Magpie
flew away without another word.

"I'm glad she's gone," said the little rabbit to himself, and just then Bobbie Red-
vest began to sing:

> "Every day a little work,
>   Every day a song,
> Every day a kindly word
>   Helps us all along."

And after that he picked up a crumb and
said:

"Good morning, little rabbit. Don't forget to feed the canary."

"Gracious me!" exclaimed the little
bunny, "I almost forgot!" And wouldn't

it have been dreadful if he had, for little
Miss Canary couldn't get out of her gold
cage and look for worms like all the wild
birds can, you know.

Well, when the little rabbit had finished
his work, he hopped out to the Sunny
Meadow where Mr. Merry Sun was making
the buttercups grow more yellow every day,
and the daisies whiter.

MRS. ORIOLE'S MIRROR

Oh, Mrs. Cow has a little bell
Tied to her neck with a string,
And every time she shakes her head
It gives a ting-a-ling-ling.

"HELLOA, little rabbit," said Ducky Waddles. "I guess I'll go down to the Old Duck Pond and take a swim." So off he went, wabbly, wabbly, on his big yellow feet, and pretty soon he saw Granddaddy Bullfrog on his log. The old gentleman frog was feeling very fine this lovely spring morning, for he had just eaten thirty-three flies, and that's a pretty good breakfast, let me tell you, even if the advertisements say you must

eat shavings and cream to be perfectly
well.

"Good morning, Ducky Waddles," said
Granddaddy Bullfrog. "Have you heard
the news?"

"What news?" asked Ducky Waddles,
taking off his collar and his blue necktie before jumping into the water.

"Why, the Farmer's Boy has gone to the
city to see his old maid aunt," said Granddaddy Bullfrog with a grin. "He won't
throw stones at me now for maybe a week."

"Well, that's good news," said Ducky
Waddles. "Now I can take a swim without
worrying about my new necktie." And he
flopped into the water with a splash that
almost frightened to death a little tadpole
who was swimming close by.

"Gracious me!" said the Little Tadpole,

whose name was Tad, "if that old duck had
seen me he would have gobbled me up as
quick as a winkerty blinkerty." And then
he hid behind a water lily stem until
Ducky Waddles was far away.

Well, Ducky Waddles hadn't gone very
far before Mrs. Oriole, who had a nest like
a long white stocking on a branch of the
weeping willow tree, began to sing:

> "Swing high, swing low,
> Swing to and fro
> From the branch of the willow tree.
> But whenever I look
> In the Bubbling Brook
> Another bird looks at me."

"Ha, ha!" laughed Professor Jim Crow,
who happened to come by just then. "What
sort of a bird lives in the Bubbling Brook?"

"Well, I can tell you one thing," said

Mrs. Oriole, "she doesn't keep her feathers well combed."

And then you should have heard that wise old blackbird laugh.

"Well, when you look in the Bubbling Brook again," he said, "comb your feathers, Mrs. Oriole, and perhaps that other bird will do the same."

And would you believe it, that's just what happened? But how Professor Jim Crow knew it I'm sure I don't know, unless his wife had a vanity bag with a little mirror in it, as all the ladies do nowadays who don't vote, I'm told.

AN AIRSHIP RIDE

WELL, all of a sudden, as Mrs. Oriole combed her yellow curls—beg pardon, I mean feathers—Little Jack Rabbit heard a voice say, quite close to his ear, "Hello!" And when he looked around he saw his friend the Jay Bird perched on a bramble branch.

"How did you get here?" asked the little rabbit.

"In my airship," replied the little bird. "Don't you want to take a ride?"

"Will you wait till I finish cleaning my gold watch?" and the little rabbit set to work, and before long he could see his face

in it and the Jay Bird's too, for Mr. Merry
Sun made that little gold watch shine like
a ball of fire.

Then away went the little rabbit and the
Jay Bird, and pretty soon they were flying
over the Sunny Meadow, over the treetops
and over the steeples, and over the houses
and over the peoples!

Well, sir, it wasn't very long before they
were far, far away from the Shady Forest,
and then the little rabbit said: "Don't go
too far, Mr. Jay Bird, for mother will worry
if I don't get home in time for supper." And
just then up came the American Eagle with
a big flag in his beak and seven silver stars
on the tips of his tail feathers.

"O come with me and I'll show you where
  I've a nest on the mountain high in the air;

> It's a lonely place, but it's home for me,
> With Mrs. Eagle and children three."

"Show us the way and we'll follow," said the Jay Bird, and he steered his airship after the great American Eagle, and by and by they came to his nest high up on the mountain's rocky crest.

The little rabbit hopped out and went over to say how do you do to the little eaglets, and when they showed him their Thrift Stamp Books, what do you think this generous little rabbit did? Why, he opened his knapsack and gave them each a War Saving Stamp. Wasn't that kind of him?

Then Mrs. Eagle went to the ice box for ice cream cones, and everybody had a feast, and after that the Jay Bird said it was time to go. So he and the little rabbit got into the airship and went away, and by and by they

were just above the Bramble Patch. Mrs.
Rabbit was looking out of the window, and
as soon as she saw them way up high in the
clear blue sky, she rang the supper bell, and
Cocky Doodle sang:

> "Home again, my little rabbit,
> That's the place to be.
> Only there true love and rest
> Waits for you and me."

LITTLE JACK RABBIT BOOKS

(Trademark Registered)

By DAVID CORY

Author of LITTLE JOURNEYS TO HAPPYLAND

Colored Wrappers With Text Illustrations

A new and unique series about the furred and feathered little people of the wood and meadow.

Children will eagerly follow the doings of little Jack Rabbit, who, every morning as soon as he has polished the front door knob and fed the canary, sets out from his little house in the bramble patch to meet his friends in the Shady Forest and Sunny Meadow. And the clever way he escapes from his three enemies, Danny Fox, Mr. Wicked Weasel and Hungry Hawk will delight the youngsters.

GROSSET & DUNLAP, PUBLISHERS, NEW YORK

Of course Teddy
Turtle was late.

"No Siree, I get them
for myself."

She hopped into the
Luckymobile.

"Who can it be?" whispe
ed Miss Mousie.